GW01179688

The Pharaoh's Puzzle

The Time-Traveling Kids, Volume 2

Jason Bland

Published by Jason Bland, 2024.

THE PHARAOH'S PUZZLE

First edition. November 12, 2024.

Written by Jason Bland.

CHAPTER 1

THE MYSTERIOUS SYMBOLS

Back in Eldergrove, the peaceful, everyday rhythms of village life feel strange for Emma, Liam, and Zoe after their time in medieval England. Though only a few weeks have passed, they can't shake the memory of their incredible adventure or the realization that magic and mystery truly exist. They've been visiting the village library almost daily, researching medieval artifacts and ancient history, hoping to make sense of what happened and, secretly, longing for the sundial to spark to life again.

One drizzly autumn afternoon, as Emma pores over a thick book on European history, something catches her eye. "Guys, look at this," she says, her voice barely a whisper. There, faintly overlaid on the page, are strange, ancient symbols. They're barely visible, as if someone had painted them in a thin mist. Liam and Zoe peer over her shoulder.

"What are those?" Zoe asks, squinting at the markings. "They almost look like... hieroglyphs?"

Liam nods slowly, his eyes widening. "I think you're right. They look Egyptian."

Emma, scribbling furiously, tries to capture the symbols in her notebook. But as quickly as they'd appeared, the symbols begin to fade, leaving only a trace on the page. The friends exchange uneasy looks, each of them sensing the same thing: the sundial might be calling them once again.

Hurrying through the rain, they race to the attic where they'd first discovered the sundial. As they ascend the narrow wooden staircase, their footsteps echo, blending with the soft patter of rain on the attic's old roof. The sundial sits exactly where they'd left it, yet now it feels different, as if alive with hidden energy.

When they approach, the faint glow returns, revealing an intricate line of hieroglyphs along the sundial's edge. Emma quickly starts jotting them down, and Zoe takes a quick photo with her camera. But just like in the library, the symbols begin to fade as if they're meant only to be seen briefly, a fleeting message from another world.

"What do you think it means?" Emma asks, her voice barely above a whisper.

Liam studies the symbols closely. "I think… it's some kind of invitation. A call. Like it wants us to follow these symbols to wherever they're from."

Zoe, trembling with excitement, reaches for their hands. "If we've already traveled once, maybe the sundial's showing us we're meant to go again. Are you guys ready?"

Without hesitation, they all place their hands on the sundial, the cool metal sending a slight shiver through their fingers. As the ancient symbols flash briefly one last time, the world around them begins to blur. Colors and shapes spin and twist until they're surrounded by bright, golden light and the powerful warmth of the sun.

CHAPTER 2

A LAND OF PYRAMIDS

The golden light fades, and Emma, Liam, and Zoe blink against the intense brightness. As their eyes adjust, they're awestruck by what they see. The scene before them is like something out of a history book: massive, sun-drenched pyramids tower against a blue sky, their smooth stone faces gleaming. Nearby, statues of gods with animal heads guard temple entrances, their features imposing and mysterious.

The dry desert air is stifling, and the heat presses down on them like a heavy blanket. They exchange stunned glances, each silently absorbing the truth, they're really in ancient Egypt.

"Look at that!" Zoe exclaims, pointing to a colossal statue of a sphinx with a fierce, proud face. "I never thought I'd actually see one in real life."

Liam pulls out his notebook, scribbling down details. "This is incredible. I wonder what year we're in."

A group of locals in linen robes and headcloths walks by, casting curious glances their way. Emma notices that the people seem to assume they're visitors to the kingdom, though their clothes stand out starkly against the flowing garments of the Egyptians. One boy, close to their age and dressed in the simple tunic of an apprentice, stops and looks at them curiously.

"Are you… travelers from another kingdom?" the boy asks, eyeing their clothes with interest. He introduces himself as Rami, an apprentice scribe working in the Pharaoh's palace.

Emma hesitates, unsure what to say, but Rami seems friendly, his eyes full of wonder rather than suspicion. "Yes, we're visitors, you could say," she replies, smiling.

Rami nods, then glances at the sundial Emma still clutches in her hand. "That is a strange artifact. I've never seen anything like it. Are you here on a mission?"

The trio exchanges a quick glance, knowing they can't reveal their true purpose. "Sort of," Liam says. "We're… here to learn more about Egypt. Is there any place you recommend we visit?"

Rami beams. "Then you must come to the Pharaoh's court! He welcomes foreigners and scholars from all over. His palace is the grandest place in Egypt, full of treasures and knowledge." Rami gestures towards a distant complex of stone buildings with colorful banners flying in the hot breeze.

Emma, Liam, and Zoe follow Rami through bustling marketplaces, where merchants sell everything from spices to jewelry. The scents of cinnamon and incense fill the air, mingling with the hum of people bargaining and calling out to customers. The kids try not to stare, but everything is so mesmerizing, the intricately carved pottery, the vibrant fabrics, and the towering obelisks etched with hieroglyphs.

As they near the palace, Rami leans in and whispers, "But be careful. There are whispers in the palace of a mysterious artifact, one that some say has the power to change Egypt forever. Only those close to the Pharaoh know the full story."

Emma's heart skips a beat. Could this artifact be linked to their journey? The thought fills her with excitement but also dread, especially if Balthazar is already here, seeking the same power.

They reach the Pharaoh's palace, a grand structure with tall, sandstone pillars and carvings of gods and pharaohs that tower above them. Guards in ornate helmets stand at the entrance, their spears crossed. Rami explains their visit, and after a quick glance, the guards nod, allowing them inside.

The palace interior is a maze of grand hallways, statues, and painted walls depicting scenes of battles, gods, and pharaohs. Everything glows with a golden light from torches set in brass holders along the walls. The ceiling is painted like the night sky, with stars twinkling in the flickering light.

Rami guides them into the central court, where a figure sits on a raised platform surrounded by advisors and guards. It's Pharaoh Akhenaten himself, a young ruler who, despite his youth, has an aura of strength and wisdom. His eyes are sharp, observing everything with a calm intensity. Beside him sits a box, decorated with the same hieroglyphs that had appeared on their sundial.

Emma nudges Liam and whispers, "That box, those are the same symbols we saw!"

Liam's eyes widen as he takes in the box's intricate carvings, realizing that this must be the artifact.

The children freeze as Pharaoh Akhenaten's gaze falls upon them, sharp and discerning. Rami steps forward, bowing respectfully, and gestures to his three companions.

"Great Pharaoh," Rami says, "these travelers are from a distant land. They seek knowledge and bring respect to your kingdom."

The Pharaoh tilts his head, his expression unreadable, before his attention shifts to Emma, who clutches the sundial tightly in her hands. His eyes narrow slightly, intrigued by the artifact. "What is that in your hands, young traveler?"

Emma feels the weight of his gaze, her pulse quickening. She hesitates, choosing her words carefully. "It is... a family heirloom. We study artifacts from many lands, and we were drawn here by the symbols it bears. They match those on your box."

Pharaoh Akhenaten's expression shifts, a glint of interest in his eyes. He gestures to the puzzle box beside him, decorated with hieroglyphs similar to those

Emma, Liam, and Zoe had seen on the sundial. "This box," the Pharaoh says, his voice low, "holds secrets entrusted to my line by the gods. Many have tried to unlock its mysteries, but only those with pure hearts and wise minds may attempt it."

Emma, Liam, and Zoe exchange glances, feeling the weight of his words. They sense that this puzzle box is connected to their quest, and a thrill runs through them at the possibility of unlocking its secrets.

The Pharaoh rises, his presence commanding, and speaks to the children directly. "You may stay in my palace," he says. "But be warned: there are those who seek this box for themselves, men who hide in the shadows, drawn by greed and ambition. You must be cautious."

The children bow in gratitude, understanding the Pharaoh's warning. As they leave the court, Rami whispers urgently, "There's a story among the scribes that this box was created by the great architect Imhotep himself, to safeguard a powerful secret. But no one truly knows what lies inside, only that it holds knowledge that could shape Egypt's future."

The trio's minds whirl with excitement and unease. Could this artifact be the reason the sundial brought them here? And if so, what danger awaits them?

Later, as they settle into their quarters within the palace, Emma, Liam, and Zoe huddle together to discuss their next steps. They now know that Balthazar could be lurking nearby, seeking the same artifact. The sundial may have given them clues, but they'll need more than luck to solve the mystery before he does.

Just as they're deep in conversation, a shadow falls across their room. They look up to find a tall figure with piercing eyes standing in the doorway, it's Balthazar, his face twisted in a smile that's both menacing and triumphant.

"Ah, my dear young friends," he says smoothly. "I see you're once again meddling in matters far beyond your understanding. But this time, I'm afraid you're out of your depth."

The kids' hearts pound as they realize they're face-to-face with their greatest foe, right in the heart of ancient Egypt. They brace themselves, knowing they're in for the adventure of a lifetime.

CHAPTER 3

THE FIRST CLUE

The tension in the air is thick as Balthazar steps into the room, his dark cloak trailing behind him like a shadow. His eyes glint with triumph, and the kids feel the weight of his calculating gaze. Emma clenches her hands, fighting the urge to step back, while Liam and Zoe position themselves protectively beside her.

"What do you want, Balthazar?" Liam asks, trying to sound braver than he feels.

Balthazar's smirk grows. "Oh, I think you already know. You three have a habit of getting in my way, but that ends here. I'm here for the box, and I'll stop at nothing to claim its secrets."

Emma's mind races. She knows they need to keep Balthazar from the Pharaoh's puzzle box at all costs. But they don't yet know its mysteries or how to protect it. She glances at Zoe and Liam, hoping they're all thinking the same thing: they need a plan, and fast.

"Good luck with that, Balthazar," Zoe says, forcing confidence into her voice. "We're not afraid of you."

Balthazar's smile fades, replaced by a look of warning. "Be careful with your words, little one. You may find yourself regretting them." With a final, icy glare, he turns and leaves, his footsteps echoing down the palace corridors.

Once he's gone, the kids release the breaths they didn't realize they'd been holding. Rami, who had quietly slipped into the room during the confrontation, finally speaks up, his face pale. "That man... he's dangerous. I don't know who he is, but the scribes have whispered of a stranger in the palace, one who is feared by many."

Emma nods. "That's Balthazar. He's been following us and wants to control the secrets of time itself. If he gets his hands on the Pharaoh's puzzle, there's no telling what he'll do with its power."

They quickly decide to find the puzzle box, convinced that it holds clues to stopping Balthazar and understanding why the sundial brought them here. With Rami as their guide, they slip through the winding palace corridors, avoiding guards and advisors, until they reach the grand chamber where the box is kept.

They enter cautiously, the room dimly lit by torches that flicker and cast shadows over the stone walls. The box rests on a pedestal in the center of the room, adorned with golden carvings of Egyptian gods and mysterious symbols that seem to shift and change in the firelight.

Liam steps closer, his eyes glued to the intricate hieroglyphs on the box's surface. "Look, these symbols are similar to the ones we saw on the sundial," he whispers. "They must be connected."

Rami nods, whispering, "It's said that the box contains a map to something called the 'Pharaoh's Secret,' a knowledge so powerful that it could change the fate of Egypt."

Emma reaches out and gently touches the box's surface, feeling the cool metal under her fingers. She traces one of the symbols, and suddenly, with a soft click, the box shifts, revealing a hidden compartment containing a small golden key and a scroll wrapped in delicate silk.

Excited, Zoe carefully unrolls the scroll. The ancient papyrus is covered in faded ink, detailing a riddle:

"To unlock the Pharaoh's hidden might, You must find the stones of light. Scattered near the Nile's flow, Guarded where the shadows grow."

Emma, Liam, and Zoe exchange intrigued glances, and Rami whispers, "The Nile... that's where many ancient temples lie. Perhaps one of them holds these 'stones of light'?"

The kids realize they've found their first clue. But just as they start to plan their next move, they hear footsteps approaching the chamber. They hide behind a massive column, clutching the scroll and the key, and watch as Balthazar strides into the room.

He examines the box closely, frustration evident in his movements. "Where did they go?" he mutters, realizing the kids have likely already taken the clue.

The friends hold their breath, praying Balthazar doesn't spot them. After a tense moment, he storms out, his frustration echoing in his heavy footsteps.

They exchange relieved glances once he's gone, knowing they've just barely escaped. They have the first clue, but Balthazar is close behind. With Rami's help, they slip back into the palace's quieter corridors, their minds racing.

"We have to find those stones," Emma says, her voice determined. "If the sundial brought us here, there's a reason. This must be our mission."

Liam nods, clutching the golden key. "And we need to stay one step ahead of Balthazar."

Together, the four of them begin to plan their journey to the Nile, knowing that the adventure, and danger, has only just begun.

CHAPTER 4

SECRETS OF THE NILE

At dawn, Emma, Liam, Zoe, and Rami slip out of the palace with the golden key and the scroll, determined to reach the Nile before Balthazar catches on. The air is cool and still as they make their way past the outer walls of the city, leaving the bustling markets and towering statues behind.

Their journey leads them to a path that follows the Nile, where the water glistens in the early morning sun. Birds circle above, and in the distance, they can see farmers tending to crops along the river's edge. The kids feel a thrill of excitement mixed with nerves, knowing they're headed into the unknown.

As they walk, Rami explains more about the temples that line the Nile. "Many of these temples are protected by priests and guarded by statues of the gods," he says. "Only those who show respect and wisdom are allowed to enter."

Emma nods, clutching the scroll. She can't help but feel that the words of the riddle are guiding them. *'Scattered near the Nile's flow, guarded where the shadows grow,'* she repeats in her mind, searching the landscape for anything that might match the clue.

After hours of walking, they reach a fork in the river where ancient stones form a path toward a towering temple half-hidden by thick reeds and overgrown vines. It's a secluded place, and there's an eerie silence that settles around them as they approach. The temple's entrance is guarded by two massive statues of Anubis, the jackal-headed god of the afterlife, their faces stern and watchful.

"This must be it," Liam whispers. "It feels… right."

They cautiously approach the temple's entrance, stepping carefully as if any loud noise might awaken the ancient guardians. Inside, the temple is dark and cool, the air heavy with the scent of incense. Faint carvings cover the walls, and Emma runs her fingers over the hieroglyphs, reading the symbols for "light," "eternity," and "truth."

Suddenly, a voice echoes from the shadows, startling them. "Who dares enter this sacred place?"

A priest, dressed in white linen and holding a staff adorned with a symbol of Ra, steps forward. His gaze is stern as he examines the group, his eyes lingering on the scroll and the key Emma holds.

Rami bows deeply, and the others follow suit. "We are travelers, seeking knowledge and honor," Rami says respectfully. "We have come to understand the secrets of this place."

The priest's expression softens slightly, but he remains cautious. "Many seek the secrets guarded here, but few are worthy. If you wish to pass, you must prove your wisdom. Answer this: What is the only thing that can reveal both truth and falsehood in equal measure?"

The friends exchange puzzled glances, each thinking furiously. Zoe's eyes light up as she whispers, "The light. The light reveals both what is true and what is hidden."

Emma steps forward confidently. "The answer is light."

The priest nods, a hint of approval in his expression. "You have answered well. Follow me."

He leads them deeper into the temple, through twisting corridors lined with intricate carvings that tell stories of gods and kings. Finally, they reach a small chamber at the heart of the temple. In the center of the room, atop a pedestal, sits a gleaming white stone, smooth and polished, radiating a soft, ethereal glow.

Emma gasps, feeling an intense pull toward the stone. She remembers the riddle's words: *'You must find the stones of light.'* This must be one of them.

The priest holds up his hand. "The stone is a gift from the gods, bestowed upon those who seek wisdom. It is not to be taken lightly."

Emma, Zoe, and Liam exchange a silent look of agreement. They've come this far; they know they must accept the responsibility that comes with the stone. Slowly, Emma reaches out, her fingers grazing its cool surface. The room fills with a warm, pulsing light, and a sense of clarity and purpose fills her heart.

As she lifts the stone, an image flashes in her mind: a map of Egypt, with symbols highlighting other temples and sacred sites along the Nile. She understands immediately, each of these places holds a stone like this, each one a piece of the Pharaoh's puzzle.

"Thank you," Emma says, bowing to the priest. "We will guard it well."

The priest nods solemnly. "The path you follow is fraught with danger. Be wary of those who would use this power for ill."

With the stone safely in Emma's bag, the kids and Rami make their way out of the temple. The sunlight feels sharper, the air fresher, as they emerge back into the warmth of the Egyptian afternoon. But their relief is short-lived.

Across the clearing, Balthazar stands waiting, a sinister smile on his face.

"So, you found the first stone," he says, his voice dripping with satisfaction. "It seems I underestimated you." His hand reaches toward his cloak, where a glint of metal catches the sun.

Emma steps back, clutching the stone protectively. "You'll never get this, Balthazar. We won't let you use it."

Balthazar's smile doesn't falter. "We'll see about that, my dear." He steps closer, his movements slow and calculated. The kids know they're in trouble, with no easy escape route.

Just then, Rami whispers urgently, "Follow me!" and darts toward a path hidden by the reeds. The kids follow, sprinting as fast as they can, the sound of Balthazar's footsteps growing fainter behind them. They don't stop running until they're far from the temple, breathless and exhilarated.

"Let's get back to the palace," Liam says, holding the map Emma sketched from her vision. "We have more stones to find, and we can't waste any time."

As they make their way back, their determination grows. They have the first stone of light, and now, a map to guide them. But they also know that Balthazar won't stop until he has what he wants. Their mission has only just begun.

CHAPTER 5

THE TEMPLE OF SHADOWS

Back at the palace, Emma, Liam, Zoe, and Rami gather in a quiet corner, examining the map Emma saw in her vision. Each marked location represents a temple along the Nile, and they know that finding the remaining stones of light will lead them closer to the secrets within the Pharaoh's puzzle box.

"We got lucky with the first stone," Liam says. "But Balthazar is only going to get more aggressive."

Emma nods, tracing a finger over the map. "The next temple looks like it's deeper into the desert, near a place called the Temple of Shadows."

Rami's eyes widen. "I've heard stories of that place. It's said to be cursed, protected by shadowy figures that appear when the sun is at its highest. Few who enter the temple ever return."

Zoe swallows, her excitement mingling with fear. "Well, if the next stone is there, we don't have a choice. We can't let Balthazar get to it first."

With a sense of urgency, the group sets out at dawn, following the Nile's winding banks and moving further into the desert. The heat intensifies as the sun climbs higher, and the sand seems to stretch endlessly around them, shimmering under the sun's relentless glare.

After hours of walking, they reach a towering structure half-buried in sand, the Temple of Shadows. Its massive stone pillars are adorned with hieroglyphs that seem darker, almost as though they were painted in the blackest ink. The temple is eerie and silent, casting a long shadow across the desert sands.

"This place gives me the creeps," Liam mutters, clutching his bag tighter.

Emma takes a steadying breath. "Stay close. If we stick together, we'll be fine."

They step into the temple, and immediately the air feels colder, as if they've entered a different world. Flickering shadows dance along the walls, and the kids can't tell if it's their imaginations or something more sinister.

As they make their way through the winding corridors, they come across strange inscriptions, each one depicting scenes of darkness and light battling each other. Emma pauses, studying the hieroglyphs. "I think this temple was built to guard the balance between light and darkness," she says. "The stone we're looking for must have something to do with that balance."

Just then, a faint sound echoes from deeper within the temple, a low, whispering voice. The kids freeze, and Rami's face pales. "They say the shadows here can speak," he whispers.

Undeterred, Zoe steps forward. "Maybe it's a clue. Let's follow it."

They walk deeper, the voices growing louder, until they reach a large chamber at the heart of the temple. In the center of the room stands an altar, upon which rests a dark, polished stone emitting a faint, eerie glow. This stone, too, seems to call to Emma, just as the first one had.

But as she reaches out to take it, a sudden gust of cold wind sweeps through the room, and shadows begin to form around them, taking the shape of tall, ominous figures. The kids step back, huddling together as the shadows draw closer, their eyes glowing faintly.

One of the shadow figures speaks in a hollow voice. "Who dares to seek the stone of darkness?"

Emma musters her courage and steps forward. "We come in peace, to seek wisdom and protect the balance between light and dark. We need this stone to complete a quest set by Pharaoh Akhenaten himself."

The shadow figures seem to consider her words, and then another voice speaks. "To prove your worth, you must answer this: *When the sun is hidden, what shines in its place, a light in the darkness?*"

The kids look at each other, thinking hard. Emma's mind races, trying to think of what might represent light in the absence of the sun. Then, a thought strikes her, and she whispers, "The stars. The stars shine when the sun is hidden."

The shadows shift, and the tension in the room eases. "You have answered correctly," the voice says. "But be warned, darkness and light are two sides of the same coin. Do not let one consume the other, or chaos will follow."

The shadow figures fade, leaving the room silent once more. Emma steps forward and picks up the stone of darkness, feeling a strange mix of power and calm emanate from it. She can sense it is another piece of the puzzle, each stone representing a different part of the balance Pharaoh Akhenaten sought to protect.

"Let's get out of here before anything else shows up," Zoe whispers, her voice tinged with relief.

They quickly make their way back through the temple corridors, emerging into the bright sunlight outside. They're exhausted but triumphant, having secured the second stone. As they catch their breath, Rami notices something in the distance, a figure moving swiftly across the dunes.

"It's Balthazar!" he gasps. "He must've followed us here!"

Without hesitation, the kids sprint away from the temple, weaving through the dunes to lose Balthazar's trail. They make their way back toward the Nile, feeling the weight of their task grow heavier. They've managed to stay ahead of Balthazar for now, but they know the chase is far from over.

As they rest by the river, Emma pulls the first stone of light and the second stone of darkness from her bag, feeling the strange energy they give off when placed side by side.

"Two down, and who knows how many more to go," Liam says, trying to catch his breath.

"But we're getting closer," Emma replies, determined. "Each stone brings us closer to the Pharaoh's secret. We just have to stay ahead of Balthazar and keep going."

With renewed determination, they pack up and continue along the river, heading toward the next temple on the map, knowing that their journey is only growing more dangerous with each step.

CHAPTER 6

THE SANDS OF ILLUSION

With two stones in their possession, Emma, Liam, Zoe, and Rami feel both hopeful and anxious. Their next destination on the map is a place called the Oasis of Mirrors, a hidden spot deep within the desert. According to legend, it's a place where reality and illusion blend, where only the pure of heart can see the truth.

"An oasis sounds nice," Liam says as they trudge through the sandy terrain. "But if it's anything like the Temple of Shadows, I don't think we're in for a relaxing dip."

Emma manages a small smile, though she feels the weight of the stones in her bag, both literal and symbolic. "Let's just stay alert. Every step brings us closer to the Pharaoh's secret and to keeping it safe from Balthazar."

As they journey deeper into the desert, the temperature rises, and the landscape begins to shimmer in the heat.

Emma notices strange mirages forming in the distance: images of cities, trees, and even people flickering on the horizon before dissolving into thin air.

Finally, after hours of walking, they spot what looks like an oasis nestled between two large dunes. Tall palm trees sway in the breeze, and clear, sparkling water reflects the brilliant sky.

But as they approach, Rami stops them, his eyes narrowing. "Wait. This might not be what it seems. The Oasis of Mirrors is known to play tricks on those who enter."

Cautiously, the kids step closer, peering into the water. To their surprise, each of their reflections is slightly different. Emma's reflection looks older, with a wise but weary expression. Liam's reflection is tall and muscular, like a seasoned warrior. Zoe's wears a crown, while Rami's reflection is draped in royal robes.

"It's showing us… alternate versions of ourselves," Zoe whispers, captivated.

Emma touches the surface of the water, and her reflection ripples, replaced by a new image. This time, she sees a pathway under the water, leading somewhere unknown.

"This must be part of the challenge," she says. "We need to enter the water to find the next stone. But we have to stay focused, or we might get lost in the illusions."

One by one, they step into the oasis, the water cool and soothing after their hot journey. But as soon as they're fully submerged, the world around them shifts. They find themselves in a cavernous underwater space filled with light and shadow, surrounded by shimmering walls that reflect countless versions of themselves.

Each version moves independently, some beckoning them forward, others warning them to turn back. It's dizzying, and Emma feels her head spin as she tries to focus.

"Stay close!" she calls out. "Don't lose sight of each other."

But the illusions grow stronger. Emma catches glimpses of her friends drifting toward different paths, led astray by strange visions. She sees Zoe stepping toward an image of herself wearing a crown, and Liam reaching out to a warrior version of himself.

"Guys, stop! It's not real!" Emma shouts, snapping them back to reality. She grabs Liam's arm, pulling him away from his reflection, and Zoe returns to her side, shaken.

"I almost… it felt so real," Zoe whispers.

"We can't let the illusions distract us," Rami says, his voice steady. "We have to find the stone and get out of here."

As they push forward, the water begins to grow darker, and the path narrows, leading them to a small alcove at the heart of the oasis. There, sitting on a pedestal surrounded by glowing symbols, is a third stone, a deep blue one that seems to pulse with a calming energy.

Emma reaches out, but just as her fingers brush the stone, a rumbling sound echoes through the water. The shimmering walls around them begin to ripple, and the images in the mirrors shift, twisting into darker, distorted versions of themselves.

Out of the reflections step shadowy duplicates of each of them, their expressions cold and hostile. The duplicates move toward them, blocking their path back to the surface.

"What… what are they?" Zoe stammers, her eyes wide with fear.

"They're illusions… but they feel real," Emma says, feeling a chill run down her spine.

The duplicates mimic their movements, and Emma realizes they'll have to think differently if they're to escape. She takes a deep breath, focusing on the stone in her hand. An idea sparks.

"Everyone, close your eyes," she says. "Remember who you are, who we really are. These illusions can't harm us if we don't believe in them."

Her friends nod, closing their eyes, and together they hold hands, concentrating on their true selves. Gradually, the shadowy duplicates begin to fade, losing their substance until they vanish completely. When Emma opens her eyes, the cavern is empty, and they are alone once more.

Relieved, Emma places the blue stone in her bag, feeling its calming presence beside the other stones. "That was too close," she says, breathing heavily. "These stones are getting harder to find, and Balthazar will only get more determined to stop us."

They make their way back to the surface, emerging from the water and blinking in the bright sunlight. The oasis behind them looks still and peaceful, hiding its true nature from any unsuspecting traveler.

"I hope we don't have to deal with illusions again," Liam mutters, wringing water from his shirt.

Emma just smiles, though her thoughts are already focused on the next temple on the map. They have three stones now, and she can feel the puzzle's pieces starting to come together.

As they rest by the edge of the oasis, Rami points to a far-off shape on the horizon, a figure moving slowly but steadily toward them. Even from a distance, they can tell it's Balthazar, his determination as unyielding as the desert itself.

"We need to move," Emma says urgently. "If he catches up to us here, we'll be trapped."

With a renewed sense of urgency, they gather their things and set off toward the next temple, ready to face whatever challenges lie ahead. They know now that each stone will demand more from them, and that Balthazar will stop at nothing to claim the Pharaoh's secret for himself.

CHAPTER 7

THE KEEPER OF THE FLAME

After escaping the Oasis of Mirrors, Emma, Liam, Zoe, and Rami push on through the desert, the weight of the three stones in Emma's bag growing heavier with each step. The map points to a place far ahead: an ancient structure known as the Temple of the Sun, said to be guarded by a mysterious figure called the Keeper of the Flame. According to the stories, only those who prove their courage can enter the temple and unlock its secrets.

As the kids walk, the sun begins to set, casting long shadows across the sand. The temperature drops, and the desert takes on a strange, quiet stillness. They reach a small cliff and pause, looking out over the landscape. In the distance, they see the Temple of the Sun, half-hidden in the shadows of the encroaching night.

"There it is," Emma whispers, awe in her voice. The temple's massive stone columns and intricate carvings are barely visible in the fading light, but they can feel its presence, ancient and imposing.

"It's even more impressive than the last ones," Zoe says. "But I bet the challenge inside won't be easy."

As they approach the temple, the entrance glows faintly, casting a warm light across the sand. Standing before the door is a figure draped in dark, flowing robes, holding a staff topped with a flame that flickers despite the lack of wind. The Keeper of the Flame looks up as they approach, his face hidden beneath a hood.

"You seek the fourth stone," the Keeper says in a low, echoing voice. "But this temple guards the secrets of the sun, and only those who possess true courage may enter. Are you ready to prove yourselves?"

Emma steps forward, feeling a mixture of fear and resolve. "We're ready. We've come this far, and we won't give up now."

The Keeper studies her for a moment, then raises his staff. The flame at the top flares, casting strange shadows across the ground. "Then enter," he says. "But beware, within these walls, your greatest fears will take shape. You must face them if you wish to continue."

With a nod, the kids step inside, their hearts pounding. The air inside the temple is warm and heavy, and the walls are lined with intricate carvings depicting the sun's journey across the sky. As they walk deeper into the temple, the light from the Keeper's flame fades, leaving them in near-total darkness.

Suddenly, the ground trembles, and the walls around them seem to shift. Shadows gather, suddenly, the ground trembles, and the walls around them seem to shift, creating a maze of dark passageways. Strange, echoing sounds fill the air, whispers, footsteps, even faint, ghostly laughter. The kids look at each other, their faces tense, but they press forward, each step a test of their courage.

As they move deeper into the maze, the whispers grow louder, and Emma feels a chill creep up her spine. The shadows on the walls seem to shift, taking on familiar shapes and forms. Suddenly, one of the shadows stretches out, forming into a tall figure, a shadowy version of her father, looking disappointed and distant.

"Emma, you'll never be able to protect the stones," the figure says, its voice low and haunting. "You're not strong enough."

Emma gasps, momentarily frozen by the words. The fear of failing her friends and letting the stones fall into Balthazar's hands feels all too real. But as the shadow steps closer, she remembers the courage that brought her this far. She closes her eyes, takes a deep breath, and says firmly, "You're just an illusion. I won't let fear stop me."

The shadow figure fades, and the path forward becomes clear once more. She glances at her friends, who are facing their own fears: Zoe stares down a vision of herself lost and alone, while Liam faces a shadow of himself falling behind, unable to keep up. Rami stands frozen before a vision of his family in danger, unable to help them.

"Guys, remember what we've already overcome," Emma calls out. "These fears aren't real! We're stronger together."

Hearing her words, Zoe, Liam, and Rami find the strength to break free from their illusions. They shake off the fear, focusing on the determination that brought them to the Temple of the Sun in the first place. One by one, the shadowy figures disappear, leaving only the four of them standing in the silent darkness.

"Thanks, Emma," Zoe says, giving her a shaky smile. "That… that was intense."

Emma nods, gripping her bag tightly. "We can do this. We just have to keep going."

As they push forward, they reach a circular chamber at the heart of the temple. In the center of the room stands a pedestal holding the fourth stone, a brilliant, fiery red gemstone that pulses with a warm, almost comforting glow. The stone feels alive, radiating a powerful energy that fills the room.

Emma steps forward, but before she can reach the stone, the Keeper of the Flame appears, his staff raised high. "To claim the stone, you must answer this: *What lights the way when courage falters, and fear seeks to take hold?*"

The kids exchange glances, thinking hard. They remember the fears they faced, the illusions that tried to hold them back. And then, Emma realizes the answer.

"Hope," she says confidently. "When courage falters, it's hope that keeps us going."

The Keeper's flame flares brightly, and he nods approvingly. "You have answered wisely," he says. "Take the stone, and may its light guide you."

Emma reaches out, her hand closing around the fiery red stone. The warmth spreads through her fingers, filling her with a renewed sense of purpose. She places it with the other stones in her bag, feeling the weight of their mission but also the strength of her friends by her side.

As they leave the temple, the Keeper's voice echoes after them. "Remember, the journey is not over. Ahead lies darkness that only true unity can withstand. Go forth with hope, and trust in each other."

Outside the temple, the first light of dawn begins to break over the horizon, casting a soft glow across the desert. The kids take a moment to rest, their spirits lifted by the triumph of facing their fears and claiming the fourth stone. But they know they can't stop for long; Balthazar is still on their trail, and the final pieces of the puzzle await.

Emma pulls out the map, her eyes scanning the final destinations. "Next stop is the Temple of the Moon," she says. "But we'll have to stay alert. Balthazar's getting closer every day."

With the fourth stone in their possession and their resolve stronger than ever, they set off toward the Temple of the Moon, ready to face whatever challenges await in their quest to protect the Pharaoh's secrets.

CHAPTER 8

ALLIES OF THE DESERT

The dawn's light fades behind them as the group makes their way toward the Temple of the Moon. They've barely rested, but adrenaline pushes them forward, knowing Balthazar could be only hours behind. The Temple of the Moon is rumored to lie hidden within the jagged hills ahead, accessible only under the light of a crescent moon.

As they walk, Emma studies the map closely. "The temple should be somewhere around here," she murmurs, frowning. But the barren landscape offers few clues. Rocks and shadows stretch in every direction, with no sign of the hidden temple.

Liam squints at the hills, then stops abruptly. "Did you hear that?" he whispers, motioning for everyone to stay silent. A soft rustling sound, almost like sand shifting, drifts toward them from behind a large rock formation.

Suddenly, a figure emerges from the shadows. A woman in flowing robes, her face partially covered, approaches them cautiously. Her eyes, piercing and wise, reveal a deep knowledge of the desert.

"Who are you?" Emma asks, taking a protective step forward.

The woman raises her hands in peace. "My name is Amara," she says, her voice calm and steady. "I am a guardian of the desert and a protector of the ancient secrets. I've watched you since you entered the oasis, and I know of the stones you carry. Balthazar seeks them, but he does not understand their true power. Nor does he realize the consequences if he tries to use them for his own gain."

Emma exchanges a look with her friends, feeling a surge of relief. They've been cautious about who to trust, but something in Amara's presence feels reassuring, as if she's meant to be part of their journey.

"You know about Balthazar?" Rami asks.

Amara nods gravely. "He has been after these stones for years, hoping to unlock their secrets for himself. But he does not understand that these stones are bound by ancient magic. To use them recklessly would unleash forces even he cannot control."

She gestures for them to follow, leading them to a hidden alcove tucked between the rocks. There, she lights a small fire, and they sit around it, feeling the warmth in the cool desert morning.

"Tell me," Amara says, her gaze sweeping over each of them. "What drives you to protect these stones, knowing the dangers that lie ahead?"

Emma hesitates, then speaks honestly. "We didn't set out to protect ancient magic," she admits. "We just wanted to help Rami, to find answers about his family's connection to the Pharaoh's secret. But along the way, we realized that we can't let someone like Balthazar get his hands on this power."

Amara's eyes soften. "Courage often finds those who least expect it," she says. "And fate has chosen you for a reason. But remember, you are stronger together than alone. The stones respond to unity, to a shared purpose. Balthazar's weakness is his desire to control, to take power for himself. You must use your strengths as a team if you hope to complete this journey."

Amara reaches into a small pouch at her side and pulls out a delicate silver amulet, engraved with symbols that glow faintly in the firelight. "This will guide you to the

Temple of the Moon. It only appears when the moonlight touches it, and it will show you the way forward."

Emma takes the amulet with a grateful smile, feeling its cool surface warm in her hand. "Thank you, Amara," she says. "We won't forget this."

Amara gives them a final, encouraging nod. "Remember, you are never alone in this journey. The ancient guardians watch over you, and their wisdom will light your path. Now go, and may the light of the moon guide you."

As they bid Amara farewell, Emma clutches the amulet, feeling its faint hum as they continue toward the Temple of the Moon. Just as the first stars appear in the night sky, a sliver of moonlight illuminates the amulet, casting a faint blue glow that points them toward a narrow path hidden between the hills.

The kids follow the light of the amulet, feeling its energy strengthen with each step. The landscape around them shifts, the hills seeming to open up to reveal a vast, rocky valley bathed in moonlight. At the far end of the valley stands the Temple of the Moon, its stone walls gleaming with an otherworldly silver light.

Emma looks at her friends, their faces reflecting both awe and determination. "This is it," she says quietly. "We're close."

They approach the temple, the amulet's glow fading as they reach the entrance. Inside, moonlight filters through small openings in the walls, illuminating strange symbols and carvings of animals, stars, and celestial patterns.

As they step inside, they're filled with a sense of peace, as if the temple itself welcomes them. Yet, they know that the final tests to obtain the fifth stone await within its walls.

CHAPTER 9

THE PATH OF THE MOON

The Temple of the Moon looms above them, its stone walls shimmering in the faint glow of moonlight. As the kids step inside, a sense of calm and purpose fills the air. The walls are carved with intricate patterns, swirling like waves, each line telling the story of the stars, the night, and the secrets held by the moon.

Emma, clutching Amara's amulet, feels the weight of their journey so far and glances at her friends. "We've come this far. Let's stay together and stay sharp."

The path within the temple is lit by moonlight spilling through cracks and openings high above, casting gentle beams on the stone floor. The glow reveals a set of stepping stones across a shallow, silvery pool. Etched onto the floor near the pool is a single line of ancient script.

Rami kneels to read the symbols aloud. "Only those who follow the light of the moon shall find the stone."

"Follow the light?" Liam repeats, looking around. "But there's barely enough light to see where we're going."

Emma holds up the amulet, and the faint glow intensifies, casting a beam toward the stepping stones. "I think this is what it means," she says, her eyes lighting up. "We have to step where the light touches."

One by one, they step onto the stones illuminated by the amulet's glow, trusting its guidance as they cross the pool. Each stone feels cool underfoot, and as they move further, the air around them grows colder, almost as if the temple itself is testing their resolve.

When they reach the other side, they find themselves in a circular room. In the center stands a massive stone pedestal with a gleaming, pale-blue gemstone, the fifth stone. Its surface glimmers with shades of silver and blue, as if reflecting the night sky itself.

Emma takes a step forward, but before she can touch the stone, a low rumble fills the room. The pedestal begins to sink into the floor, and four stone statues surrounding the room slowly come to life, their eyes glowing faintly in the moonlight.

"What's happening?" Zoe exclaims, grabbing Emma's arm.

The statues, each shaped like an animal, a wolf, an owl, a snake, and a deer, begin to circle the room, their footsteps echoing ominously. The wolf lets out a soft growl, and the owl's eyes gleam with intelligence, as if testing the kids' intentions.

"I think these guardians want us to prove we're worthy," Rami says, his voice steady but cautious. "They're here to protect the stone from anyone untrustworthy."

Emma nods, taking a deep breath. "We've come this far because we care about protecting these stones, not using them for power. We have to show them that we're here to protect their secrets."

Slowly, she walks forward, her hands open and her posture calm. The wolf statue moves closer, its stone gaze fixed on her. Emma feels a jolt of fear but forces herself to stand her ground, meeting the wolf's eyes with steady determination.

"We're here to protect the stones," she says clearly. "We won't let Balthazar take them, or let anyone misuse them."

The wolf's eyes flash, and then it bows its head slightly before stepping back into place. The other statues follow suit, each returning to their original position as if acknowledging her words. The pedestal rises once more, and the blue gemstone glows brighter, inviting Emma to take it.

With a deep breath, she reaches out and lifts the stone, feeling its cool surface pulse with a gentle energy. As she holds it, a vision fills her mind, a path leading from the desert to a vast, dark forest, illuminated by a faint, mysterious glow.

The vision fades, and Emma looks at her friends, excitement flickering in her eyes. "We've got the fifth stone. And I think I know where we're headed next, the Temple of Shadows."

As they exit the Temple of the Moon, Emma clutches the blue stone tightly, feeling a newfound confidence. She knows the next leg of their journey will be the hardest yet, but with five stones secured and their mission clearer than ever, they're ready to face whatever lies ahead.

CHAPTER 10

INTO THE SHADOWS

With the fifth stone safely in Emma's bag, the group leaves the Temple of the Moon behind, making their way through the desert under the stars. The air is cooler now, a chill that seems to seep into their bones, and the silence feels heavier, as if the night itself is watching them.

They walk until dawn, and as the sun rises, Emma pulls out the map and examines it closely. The vision she had in the temple was clear, a dark, dense forest filled with shadows. And according to the map, the Temple of Shadows lies deep within the Forest of Sable, known for its thick canopy and eerie silence.

"We'll need to head west to reach the forest," she says, pointing out the route. "It's at least a day's walk from here."

As they move onward, exhaustion starts to set in. Their journey has been long, and the dangers have been constant. But the thought of Balthazar getting his hands on the stones keeps them focused. After several hours, they finally reach the edge of the forest, its towering trees looming before them, their branches intertwining to form a near-impenetrable canopy. Sunlight barely filters through, casting the ground in an eerie half-light.

"This place is... unsettling," Zoe whispers, hugging herself as she peers into the shadows.

Emma nods. "Remember what Amara told us. We're stronger together. No matter what we face in there, we stick close and look out for each other."

They step into the forest, the silence pressing in around them like a thick blanket. Every sound, the crack of a twig, the rustle of leaves, seems amplified in the eerie stillness. Emma leads the way, her grip on the map tightening as they follow the faint trail deeper into the woods.

Hours pass, and the deeper they go, the darker it becomes. Strange shadows move among the trees, and every now and then, they catch glimpses of movement just beyond their line of sight, figures that seem to melt into the shadows whenever they look directly at them.

Suddenly, a low growl echoes through the trees, and they freeze, their eyes wide as they scan the darkness. A pair of glowing yellow eyes appears, followed by another, and another. Three shadowy figures with wolf-like shapes step into view, their eyes gleaming with an intelligence that's both mesmerizing and terrifying.

Rami swallows, his voice barely a whisper. "Are they… real?"

Emma steps forward, meeting the creatures' gaze. "They're guardians, just like in the Temple of the Moon," she says, trying to keep her voice steady. "They're here to test us."

One of the wolves steps forward, its gaze fixed on Emma, as if reading her thoughts. Then, it lets out a soft, almost mournful howl, and a faint image appears in Emma's mind, a memory of her first time exploring the woods near her home, feeling the thrill of adventure and discovery.

The wolf looks at her expectantly, and Emma realizes it's asking for something deeper: it wants to see the essence of who she is, her truest intentions.

She closes her eyes, focusing on the reason she and her friends have come this far. She thinks of her family, of wanting to protect the stones so no one else can misuse them, and of the promise they made to Rami's family to honor the Pharaoh's legacy. She opens her eyes, her gaze steady.

"We're here to protect these stones," she says quietly but firmly. "Not for power, but to keep their secrets safe."

The wolf's eyes soften, and with a nod, it steps back, allowing them to pass. The other wolves watch them intently but make no move to stop them. Slowly, they vanish into the shadows, leaving only the faint rustle of leaves behind.

The group presses on, their footsteps muffled by the thick carpet of leaves underfoot. Finally, they reach a small clearing where an ancient, crumbling structure stands, the Temple of Shadows. Its stone walls are covered in thick vines, and its entrance is dark, as if the shadows themselves cling to it.

Emma pulls out the amulet Amara gave her. It flickers faintly, casting just enough light to reveal a path leading into the temple. She looks at her friends, their faces tense but resolute.

"Are we ready?" she asks.

They nod, determination shining in their eyes. Together, they step into the temple, knowing that the challenges within will be unlike anything they've faced before.

Inside, the air is thick, almost suffocating, and the walls seem to absorb all sound. The only light comes from Amara's amulet, casting shadows that dance across the stone floor. As they move deeper into the temple, they come upon a series of symbols etched into the walls, hieroglyphs that seem to shift and change as they watch.

"These symbols... they look familiar," Rami says, his fingers tracing one of the carvings. "They're stories of the Pharaoh's life, of his greatest fears and his final triumphs."

As Rami reads, the temple seems to come alive, the walls shifting to form new passages and obstacles. A deep, resonant voice fills the air, a whisper from the shadows. "Only those who conquer their deepest fears may claim the stone."

The words send a chill down Emma's spine, and she exchanges a look with her friends. They know that the temple is about to test them in ways they can't predict.

One by one, they face their fears: Emma must confront the weight of responsibility, Zoe faces her fear of being left behind, Liam confronts his self-doubt, and Rami, his fear of losing his family's legacy. Each trial pushes them to their limits, but together, they find the strength to press on, refusing to give up.

Finally, at the heart of the temple, they find the sixth stone, a deep, dark purple gem that glows with an otherworldly light. Emma reaches out, feeling its power pulse beneath her fingertips, and as she lifts it, a new vision fills her mind, a vision of a mountain surrounded by storm clouds, lightning flashing across the sky.

She knows instinctively that it's the next part of their journey. The Temple of Storms awaits.

As they leave the Temple of Shadows, exhausted but triumphant, Emma clutches the stone tightly, feeling a renewed sense of purpose. Balthazar's presence looms closer, and the final challenges lie ahead, but with six stones now in their possession, they're closer than ever to completing their quest.

CHAPTER 11

THE MOUNTAIN OF STORMS

With the sixth stone in hand, the group leaves the dense forest and heads toward the horizon, where the mountains loom under dark, swirling clouds. Emma's vision from the Temple of Shadows guides them forward, the image of lightning illuminating a tall peak clear in her mind. This next journey promises to be both their hardest and most dangerous yet.

As they trek through rugged terrain, the air grows colder, and a stiff wind begins to blow, carrying the faint smell of rain. By the time they reach the mountain's base, the sky has turned dark and heavy, crackling with anticipation. Thunder rumbles in the distance, and the first flashes of lightning split the clouds above.

"We need to be careful," Rami says, scanning the rocky path leading upward. "This mountain is known for unpredictable storms. We don't know what we'll face up there."

The group begins their ascent, their steps careful as they navigate the narrow path that winds up the mountainside. Lightning flashes every few moments, illuminating the cliffs and revealing sheer drops just beyond the edge of the path.

As they climb higher, the storm intensifies. The wind whips around them, and rain begins to fall in sheets, making the rocks slick and treacherous. They press on, teeth clenched, eyes narrowed against the stinging rain, each step taking them closer to the summit where the Temple of Storms awaits.

Halfway up the mountain, they reach a steep incline, and the path becomes even more treacherous. Zoe slips, her foot sliding on a wet rock, but Liam grabs her arm just in time, pulling her back to safety.

"Thanks," she gasps, heart pounding.

"No problem," Liam replies with a reassuring smile. "Remember, we're stronger together."

They continue, bracing against the fierce winds, until they finally reach a ledge that opens onto a large plateau. At the far end stands the Temple of Storms, a massive stone structure built into the mountain itself.

Its walls are cracked and weathered, as if shaped by centuries of lightning strikes and raging tempests.

Emma takes a deep breath, steadying herself. "We're close. Let's go."

As they step toward the temple, a sudden bolt of lightning strikes just in front of them, sending sparks flying. A deep, booming voice echoes from the temple entrance, a voice that seems to come from the mountain itself.

"Only those who possess the courage to face the fury of the storm may enter," it warns.

The kids exchange uneasy glances. They know this challenge will push them to their limits, but they've come too far to turn back now.

Steeling themselves, they step forward into the temple. The entrance hall is dimly lit, the walls carved with symbols of swirling clouds and lightning bolts. The air inside hums with energy, crackling with the electric charge of the storm outside.

Ahead of them lies a vast chamber with a circular floor engraved with intricate patterns. At the center of the room stands a tall, crystalline obelisk that glows with a pale blue light, pulsing like a heartbeat. Surrounding the obelisk are four stone statues, each one holding a different symbol of the storm, wind, rain, thunder, and lightning.

Emma steps forward cautiously, her gaze fixed on the obelisk. "This must be the source of the storm's power," she murmurs.

As they approach, the obelisk emits a blinding flash of light, and the statues come to life, their stone faces turning toward the kids. Each statue begins to move, taking a stance that represents its element, and the chamber fills with the sound of rushing wind, booming thunder, and crackling lightning.

"We have to face each element," Rami says, his voice steady. "It's testing if we can withstand the power of the storm."

The statue representing **wind** moves first, raising its hands to summon a fierce gust that swirls around the chamber, creating a whirlwind that nearly knocks them off their feet. Emma and her friends brace themselves, holding onto each other to stay grounded, pushing forward against the wind's force until the statue finally lowers its hands, the gust fading.

Next, the **rain** statue raises its arms, and a torrent of icy water crashes down from above, soaking them and making the floor slippery. The kids hold each other's hands, forming a human chain, and carefully step across the slick floor, refusing to let the storm separate them. The rain ceases, and the statue lowers its arms.

Then, the **thunder** statue unleashes a deafening roar that shakes the walls, its vibrations strong enough to make their bones rattle. The kids close their eyes, focusing on steadying their breathing, each heartbeat syncing to the rumble of thunder. When the roar fades, they open their eyes, feeling a new strength rising within them.

Finally, the **lightning** statue raises its arms, and flashes of blinding light burst around them, crackling and sparking against the stone. Emma clutches the amulet Amara gave her, and its glow intensifies, shielding them from the worst of the lightning's fury. She holds it high, and with a final, powerful burst, the lightning dies down, leaving the chamber quiet once more.

The statues return to their original positions, and the pulsing light of the obelisk dims. A single door opens at the far end of the chamber, revealing a small room with a pedestal at its center. On the pedestal lies the seventh stone, a clear crystal that glows with the colors of the storm, shifting from blue to white to gray.

Emma steps forward and lifts the crystal, feeling a surge of energy course through her. The seventh stone's power resonates with the others in her bag, and for a brief moment, she feels connected to the mountain, the storm, and the sky above.

A vision flashes before her eyes, an image of a vast desert filled with swirling sands, and in the center, a towering pyramid unlike any they've seen before. She knows instantly that it's their next destination: the Temple of Sands. As the vision fades, Emma turns to her friends, determination sparking in her gaze. "We have the seventh stone. Now it's time for the final journey, the Temple of Sands."

They leave the Temple of Storms, exhilarated but knowing their greatest challenge lies ahead. With Balthazar hot on their trail and only one stone left to secure, they're racing against time. The fate of the stones, and the ancient magic they protect, rests on their shoulders.

CHAPTER 12

THE TEMPLE OF SANDS

The sun blazes down on the vast, endless desert as Emma, Rami, Zoe, and Liam trudge forward, sand crunching beneath their feet. The Temple of Sands lies somewhere in this barren wasteland, but its exact location remains hidden, a final mystery they must solve. Their journey has brought them here, to the edge of their endurance, and they know that Balthazar is close behind, determined to seize the stones and wield their ancient power.

Emma pulls out the map once again, scanning it carefully. "The vision showed us a pyramid surrounded by swirling sands," she says, glancing up at the endless dunes stretching out before them. "It must be nearby, but hidden somehow."

As they trek through the desert, an unnatural wind begins to pick up, swirling the sand into spirals that dance across the dunes. The sun grows hazy behind a cloud of dust, and soon, they're enveloped in a sandstorm, the grains stinging their skin and filling the air with a deafening roar. Shielding their eyes, the kids press forward, determined to reach the temple.

Suddenly, the sandstorm clears, and they find themselves standing before a massive pyramid, its stone walls gleaming under the desert sun. The Temple of Sands looms before them, majestic and mysterious, half-buried in the sands as if waiting for centuries to reveal itself.

"We made it," Rami whispers, awe in his voice.

Emma nods, gripping the bag containing the stones tightly. "This is it. The final test."

They approach the entrance of the pyramid, its dark passage leading into the unknown. As they step inside, the air grows cool and still, a stark contrast to the scorching desert outside. Flickering torches line the walls, casting shadows that dance across ancient carvings of pharaohs, gods, and mythical beasts. The deeper they go, the more the silence presses down on them, filling the air with an unspoken tension.

At the heart of the temple lies a vast chamber, its walls inscribed with symbols and hieroglyphs that seem to pulse with energy. In the center of the chamber stands an altar, and atop it rests the final stone, a brilliant golden gem that glows with the intensity of the desert sun.

But as they approach the altar, a dark figure steps out from the shadows. It's Balthazar, his eyes gleaming with a hunger for power as he blocks their path, a sinister smile spreading across his face.

"Well, well," he sneers, his voice echoing in the chamber. "You've done all the hard work for me. I'll be taking those stones now."

Emma stands her ground, her friends at her side. "We won't let you misuse their power, Balthazar," she says, her voice steady. "These stones aren't meant for you."

Balthazar laughs, raising a hand as he begins to chant. Dark energy swirls around him, crackling like electricity as it gathers in his palm. The kids feel the power of the stones within their bags, humming in response, as if urging them to stand firm against the darkness.

In unison, they step forward, each of them holding one of the stones they've gathered. As they lift the stones high, a radiant light fills the chamber, meeting

Balthazar's dark energy in a clash of power that shakes the very walls.

The light of the stones begins to form a barrier between Balthazar and the kids, pushing him back. He struggles against it, his face twisted with rage, but the stones' combined power is too strong.

Realizing he's losing, Balthazar lets out a furious scream and vanishes into the shadows, his presence fading as the light drives him away. Silence fills the chamber once again, and the kids lower their stones, their hearts pounding with relief.

With Balthazar defeated, they approach the altar, and Emma carefully places each of the seven stones around the golden gem. The moment they complete the circle, the stones emit a brilliant, blinding light, filling the chamber with warmth and peace. The ancient carvings on the walls glow in response, as if coming to life, and a deep, resonant voice fills the air.

"You have proven yourselves worthy," the voice intones. "The stones' power is safe in your hands. Return them to their rightful places, and the ancient magic shall be preserved."

As the light fades, the stones disappear, returning to their hidden places around the world. Only the golden gem remains, a symbol of their victory and the wisdom they've gained on their journey.

Emma picks up the golden gem, feeling its warmth pulsing in her hand. A new vision fills her mind, a distant land with towering ice mountains and shimmering auroras lighting up the night sky. She knows that this vision holds the key to their next adventure, a journey to the frozen north where new mysteries and ancient secrets await.

She looks at her friends, a smile spreading across her face. "Looks like our adventure isn't over yet."

They share a glance, excitement sparking in their eyes as they realize that this is only the beginning of their journey. With the golden gem in hand, they step out of the Temple of Sands, ready to face whatever new challenges the world has in store for them.

Milton Keynes UK
Ingram Content Group UK Ltd.
UKHW030944261124
451585UK00001B/261